ADVENTURES IN THE OUTBACK

SHORT STORIES SET IN REMOTE AREAS OF AUSTRALIA

GREG JESSEP

ILLUSTRATIONS BY ESTER DE BOER

Adventures in the Outback
Copyright © 2020 by Greg Jessep

Tellwell Talent
www.tellwell.ca

ISBN
978-0-2288-3971-2 (Hardcover)
978-0-2288-3970-5 (Paperback)
978-0-2288-3972-9 (eBook)

TABLE OF CONTENTS

KALPAGO

1. FILLING YOU IN

Before I tell you about my adventures, I need to fill you in on where all this takes place and tell you something about a few of the important people in my life.

My name is Charlie Jackson, I'm twelve years old and I live on a sheep and goat property, called Kalpago, with my parents and our many pets. I do my schooling at home and I am getting close to finishing my time on distance education. Next year, I'm off to boarding school.

Over the last few years, I've had a few governesses helping me with my schoolwork, mostly female backpackers from such places as Germany, Ireland and Canada. My last tutor was a man, my first male ever, and he was here for six weeks. Having tutors allows Mum to get out and help Dad on the property and avoid arguing with me about how much schoolwork I'm not doing or how sloppy the work that I do is.

Our property is quite large and for those of you who did your schooling half way through last century it is close to 90,000 acres. That's about 36,000 hectares. That all might be a bit hard to picture, so in a way you might understand, our property is a rectangle twenty-four kilometres by fifteen kilometres. The homestead is about seven kilometres from the main gravel road and thirty from town.

As you may or may not be able to imagine, when school is over for the day and on weekends, I have a fair amount of spare time. If it's raining then I'm usually on the computer playing Minecraft and if it's fine I am either on my scooter, skateboard or motorbike.

2. RAIN MISADVENTURE

Term three finished yesterday, and you guessed it, it's raining. No it's not, it's pouring. Belting down. So, Minecraft it is. Mum and Dad have gone out to Corner Dam in the Toyota to check on the inlet pipe because sometimes it gets clogged with stuff that flows in with the gushing water. When that happens, we lose some of the precious water that just spreads itself out on the nearby ground. That's great for the greening of the pasture for the animals but not so good for building up the water supply for the months or longer that we sometimes have to put up with in times of drought.

Anyway, Minecraft is going really well. I've got hold of several really good tools, some for working the land and some will definitely be used as weapons. Just when I'm getting close to finishing building up my inventory. I hear a voice that doesn't sound as if it's coming from the computer. I must have been a bit spaced out and then I realised that when I'm the only one left at the homestead, I'm supposed to keep an ear out for the two-way, just in case there is a message or a call for help. I rush out to the covered area near the cool room and pick up the handset. It's Mum. Dad has got the Toyota bogged only a short distance from the dam. This means they are about fifteen kilometres from home and in this weather that's likely to be a really tough walk. They went along the boundary fence to get there, and that's usually okay if you skirt around some of the known boggy parts. This time it didn't come off. They want me to bring the quad bike to get them back to the house. The stranded vehicle will have to wait for another day.

I remember that the middle track is much better for the smaller quad bike as there are plenty of spots where you can go around the squishy spots. You've probably guessed that living on a big property like this, and being an only child, I've become something of an expert on most of the farm machinery. That includes all the vehicles, motorbikes and the quaddie. There's only the grader to have a go at. Dad thinks I might have to wait a few years for that one.

After putting on my wet weather gear I fire up the quaddie and set off. There's not a murmur out of Jess and Chip, our two kelpies, who are keeping warm and dry inside their kennels. We did have another dog and I'll tell you about her a little later in my story.

It's very sloshy on the track and I have to dodge around quite a few of the well- known soft spots to avoid sinking out of sight, which is probably what Dad has done with the Toyota. The rain has eased a bit but it's obvious that with this amount of water lying around we should have plenty of water to keep the grass growing and the dams full for quite a while. Out here it's not unusual for us to go many months and sometimes years without good rain.

I'm having a great time sloshing through the red mud and I have to keep reminding myself that I am on a rescue mission. I can just see the top of the bogged vehicle through the trees and even though it hasn't disappeared out of sight, Dad sure has done a good job in getting it well and truly stuck. They both look pleased to see me and ask whether I had much trouble getting through. I say we will be okay getting back to the house.

It's quite a squeeze with the three of us on the quaddie. They both agree I can do the driving back to the house as I can just retrace my tracks. It isn't as much fun this time as I've got to make sure I keep them from falling off and at least a little dry. We make it all in one piece and I get a pat on the back from Dad and a big hug from Mum. Mission accomplished.

3. A FRIEND FROM SCHOOL

By the way, my motorbike is a Honda CRF 230. I've made myself a track a few hundred metres from the house. I probably should admit that parts of the track were made with Dad's help; the bucket on the front of the tractor comes in very handy when needing heaps of dirt for the jumps. I can get around the circuit pretty much at full throttle now after a few early spills. When friends visit, I get a chance to show off my skills on the Honda and there are always a few laughs when they have a turn and get a few scratches and bruises. At least then they have proof they had a red hot go.

That reminds me. This afternoon Kate arrives to spend the first week of the holidays with us. Kate is one of the other eight students doing distance education out of Broken Hill. Everyone says she's my girlfriend but really she's just someone I really like spending time with. Does that make her my girlfriend? She is a girl, and she is a friend. Enough of the mushy stuff. I've got a few things planned for the time she's at *Kalpago*. Over recent months there have been sightings of poachers on our property and maybe we can spend a bit of time trying to get some evidence against them. Now your first thought when I mentioned "poaching" was probably about them pinching our sheep or goats, but it's something a lot more valuable than that. You see, we have a few gold deposits on our property. There's not enough to set up a full scale mining operation but enough to keep a few local prospectors happy. While Mum and Dad concentrate on the sheep and goats, they also make a little extra money by asking for a small percentage of the profits made by the local gold diggers when they strike a lucky patch. This is all done as a friendly deal but people trespassing and pinching any finds is not good for the regulars and certainly not good for us.

Kate is dropped off by her parents, who are on their way for a few days in Broken Hill to catch up with family and to stock up for the weeks ahead. Out here there's no hopping down to the local supermarket or to the corner shop…you have to plan ahead and supplies are bought in huge quantities. Anyway, Kate's parents stay long enough for a cuppa and biscuits and then head off, leaving us to start our trap-the-poachers adventure. I tell Kate my plans, as sketchy as they are, and we jot down the things we might need to help us catch the intruders. The most important thing we come up with is making sure we have a camera. I have a reasonable camera but we agree we can always use our mobile phones if we get stuck. No mobile reception out here but the camera still works. Tomorrow is the day we'll put our plan into action, if we can only come up with a decent plan.

4. POACHERS, HERE WE COME!

Kate and I set out after breakfast on the quaddie. The only thing we agree on is that we need to be very careful about all this. If we get ourselves in a tricky spot there won't be any friendly adults to bail us out. Bouncing along on the quaddie, Kate has her arms around my waist for support and I have to tell you it feels kind of nice. She asks me how far it is to the gold sites and I tell her, "not very far". When you're talking about distances in the outback, most people understand that "not very far" could mean just up ahead or many kilometres. This time it is just up the track.

I select a spot with plenty of trees and low bushes to park the quaddie. Out here there aren't many of what you might call hills but there a rise in the land which has a good view of the areas where the local prospectors fire up their metal detectors and occasionally strike it lucky. We make our way to the top of this "hill" and look around to see if anyone is within sight. No one is at the moment, so we have a chance to spend some time coming up with that decent plan I was telling you about earlier.

Even though the bush isn't as thick up here, compared to where we parked the quaddie, it gives us a bit of protection from anyone who might be fossicking around down below.

Kate suggests we build some sort of a hidie place to increase our chances of not being spotted. I think this is a good idea and we set about gathering branches that have come down in the wind. I thought I was pretty clever when it comes to making cubbies but Kate is a whiz at bush huts. We soon have the ideal concealed viewing spot with several holes to see through and it's just right for taking photos of unsuspecting poachers. It doesn't seem our plan, whatever that might be, is going to be put into action today, so we head back to the bike and agree that tomorrow might be our big day.

5. NO POACHERS BUT A PICNIC

Our first day of the holidays doesn't trap any poachers but it is still special spending time with Kate and made even better by not having to think about schoolwork. After dinner we watched *Friends* on the TV. I get most of the funny lines but Kate is way ahead of me in that regard. Maybe it is true that girls mature earlier than boys. Anyway it is still enjoyable to spend time doing something like that with someone my own age instead of listening to Mum and Dad saying "I don't get it" or "what did she or he say?". Then it's off to bed to rest up for the expected big tomorrow.

We decided over breakfast to take some food with us to the hideout and also our togs and towels, just in case there is no action on the poaching front and we can picnic by the dam and maybe take a cooling off dip.

The ride to our secret hideout seemed to take forever. We have a good look around and decided after a couple of hours that today isn't going to be the big day either.

The dam, which is farther around the boundary fence and more than a stone's throw from the gold sites, is fed by a spring from underground water. If you are lucky enough to live on a property above the sub-artesian basin then there's a good chance you can tap into an endless supply of crystal clear cool water.

When we get to the dam Kate says "Wow! That looks amazing!"

We set up our picnic on a rug we brought with us and even though some of our food wasn't the most nutritious, as a parent might suggest, it looks great to both of us. We do have salad sandwiches and they are well and truly balanced out by cans of Coke, packets of chips and some chocolate bars. A while after recovering from our banquet we decided that it is certainly hot enough for a well-earned dip in the dam. We came well prepared with our togs underneath our jeans and T-shirts. Kate and I race to be the first in, and even though I don't like being beaten at most things, this is a very close thing. Let's call it a draw. This is the most fun I've had for as long as I can remember, even better than when some of the boys from school visited last year. It seems I'm getting used to the idea of having a girlfriend.

6. OUR BIG DAY ARRIVES

Yesterday was a bit of a downer as far as the poachers go, but the picnic and swimming and being with Kate certainly made up for it. Apart from our newly constructed hideout, we still don't have much of a plan if we happen to spot any intruders. Maybe making it up as we go will prove to be more exciting and maybe more successful than…well you know what they say about the best laid plans. I've heard Mum and Dad use that expression heaps of times. Sometimes I get the idea that I may have had something to do with mucking up their best laid plans. That's another story, I guess.

We make a very early start after a quick breakfast. I'm not sure about Kate but I keep wondering if the oldies will ask us what we are up to and what we might say if put on the spot. Just exploring? Showing Kate around? Luckily nothing has been said as yet. Luckily, we came well prepared with sandwiches, cans of Coke and snack bars in case another picnic and swim takes the place of spying on the intruders, if they turn up that is.

We make it to the spot where we keep the quaddie hidden and trudge up to our lookout. I look around, not only across the digging areas but also to the horizon for possible signs of vehicles. It isn't long before I spot a cloud of dust and whatever it is, it's heading our way. When you live in the outback your eyesight seems to be a bit sharper than the kids who live in the town.

It certainly is a vehicle and Kate and I agree it's a ute and when it gets closer we can clearly see there are two people in the cabin.

When they reach the nearest gate to the gold-digging areas one of them jumps out to let the vehicle through. If they aren't some of the regular prospectors, at least they do the right thing and shut the gate after themselves. The vehicle stops near a clump of trees to our right, which is several hundred metres away from the best known gold spots. I have met most of the local fossickers and from my memory these two certainly aren't any of our regular paying customers. The man who gets out of the driver's side is a big fella with tattoos on each arm and even from our vantage spot he seems to be the one in charge, pointing here and there. The second chap is as skinny as a rake and the taller of the two. He keeps looking around as if he is expecting someone to nab him at any minute. They definitely came prepared with metal detectors, small picks and shovels and bags to store anything they might be lucky enough to find. When they get closer to the area where the ground had been disturbed by others, they fire up the detectors and side by side start to cover the ground.

I tell Kate I'm fairly certain they're poachers. I've overheard Dad talking about the word around town of a couple of young blokes from down south, big-noting themselves about striking it rich. The townsfolk think they'd headed west but if these are the same two, then they must be holding up on a property somewhere in the district.

The two men are now kneeling and clawing away at the ground with their picks and shovels. I get the camera out and zoom in on the two men and take a few shots. Kate backs these up with a few on her mobile phone. What now? We can't go near the "poachers" but we can carefully make our way down to their vehicle with little chance of being seen.

Trying not to stand on anything that may crunch under our feet, we make it to the vehicle and wrack our brains as to what might be the next part of our on-the-spot plan. Almost at the same time Kate and I say, "photos!".

We take several shots of the vehicle, making sure to get a couple with the number plate in clear view. Then I remembered Dad telling this story about a prank he and his mates played on a cranky old teacher.

This was when Dad was a teenager at high school in Griffith. On the last day of school when all the teachers were inside downing a few drinks and looking forward to the Christmas school holidays, Dad and his mates sneaked up on Mr. Cranky's car and took off the petrol cap. Sugar doesn't mix too well with petrol. They then waited some distance down the road they knew the teacher would leave town on and very soon his car was approaching with a very loud knock in the engine and a very worried driver behind the wheel. Word somehow got back to town that Mr Cranky's car broke down about half way to Goolgowi and he had to be towed the rest of the way.

As it turned out it was a very expensive and nasty prank to play on someone but Dad and his mates thought it was quite okay… at least they thought so way back then.

Now without having too much of a guilty conscience, we can do the same to these two trespassers. Luckily the petrol cap is a screw-on type, unlike most of the modern cars which either require a key or are flicked open from inside.

They've locked the vehicle so we can't snoop and maybe find a clue as to who they are. I am sure they have no intention of telling Mum or Dad what they're up to and they won't be parting with any money they might make from any of their finds. But what can we use in place of the sugar that Dad and his mates used?

"The Coke!" Kate says.

Of course, soft drink is supposed to be made up mostly of sugar, so why not? I go back to the quaddie to retrieve the cans.

When I get back to Kate I carefully remove the petrol cap and Kate empties a can into the tank. I do the same and after one more can each, we figure we've done enough. We carefully put the cap back on and make our way back up to our hideout.

7. CAUGHT "GOLD-HANDED"

The two men are still digging away although they've moved to another spot. Suddenly there's excitement from below. Arms are being punched in the air and we hear yelling… "You ripper!", "Eureka!" and a few more with language I'm certainly not allowed to use.

It seems that whatever they've found may be enough, as they appear to be gathering up their detectors, tools and bags. They make their way back to the ute, with more enthusiasm than when they arrived, skipping in the air, high-fiving each other and giving a few more whoops. They must think there was no one within earshot. Little do they know they have a pair of onlookers.

I haven't realised until now that my heart is racing and thumping in my chest.

Kate says that the same is happening to her. We take a couple more photos of the pair loading up the vehicle and watched them leave Kalpago. Possibly because of their excitement they don't shut the gate behind them. I know there are no animals in this particular paddock, so that can wait for later. Besides, maybe there will be fingerprints on the gate.

With my mind racing I can't believe I even thought of something like that. Maybe I have a career in crime fighting ahead of me!

We hop on the quaddie and head back to the homestead. I drive a lot faster than I should and Kate is holding on very tightly and not giving me any hints that she is scared. I think she is just as keen as I am to tell Mum and Dad about our discovery.

I bring the four-wheeler to a dusty stop at the gate into the house area. We race inside and luckily both my parents are sitting at the kitchen table having a cuppa. Kate and I blurt out together… "Guess what we've just seen?".

I don't think they can hear what we're saying, so Mum asks that one of us speak and to take it slowly. I manage, even with my heart still pounding, to tell them what we have done and seen. Kate fills in all the gaps. We tell them about the Coke in the petrol tank. Dad immediately heads for the phone and when he starts talking I realise he is calling the police station in town. He seems to be arranging things with whoever he is talking to and when he comes off the phone he tells us to go out to the Toyota. Dad has a rifle that is registered but he doesn't go into the shed to get it.

On the way out to the main road he says he doesn't think it is a good idea to have guns around with us young'uns in the vehicle.

The poachers, unless they are intending to drive fifty or so kilometres across country through several properties, will have to skirt around our property and hit the main road back towards town. We see dust up ahead but it's difficult to figure out just how far. If the police left town at the same time we left home then we'll meet in about ten minutes. There aren't many ups and downs on the road into town but there is one rise, called Dickens Hill, and we are approaching that now. As we get to the crest, we see a vehicle pulled up on the side of the road and a police car fast approaching from the other direction.

Dad waits until the police car pulls up beside the stationery ute before slowly making his way down the hill.

It appears as if the two men, who are standing by their vehicle, are not making nuisances of themselves. I'm sure Dad wouldn't have taken us down there if there was any sign of trouble.

The men are explaining to the constable and his offsider that they have broken down and need help to get back towards town. The policemen ask them where they've come from and they say Wanaaring. They're then asked if they made a small detour off the main road into one of the properties a little way back up the road.

A chorus of "no" comes out. It's then that Kate and I step forward with Dad and camera and mobile phone at the ready. We show them the snaps we took of the vehicle and them fossicking. They claim that they thought it was okay to dig around in these outback areas. They're quickly told they have been on private property and if they had asked beforehand they may have been allowed to spend a day trying their luck.

The constable asks them if they have run out of fuel, and if that is the case, then enough is on hand to get them into town.

They say the engine appears to have given up the ghost with a loud crunching noise coming from under the bonnet.

Kate and I share a glance and sly grin and I think Dad has a smile on his face. The police indicate that the property they were on belongs to us and ask Dad if he wants to pursue the matter. Dad says if they hand over any gold they have found and promise, after getting their vehicle repaired, that they will head back to where they came from then he won't press charges. The two men seem relieved. Maybe they have learnt a valuable lesson but I have my doubts. Dad offers to tow them into town and it's fun for Kate and me as we get to ride in the police car.

We head back home in the late afternoon with one of the biggest nuggets ever found on Kalpago. We have quite a story to tell when we eventually get home to Mum later that day.

8. THE STORM AND NEW ARRIVALS

After all the excitement of catching the poachers, life settles down on Kalpago for a couple of days. Kate and I spend time exploring the property and having another picnic and swim in the dam. That afternoon a few rumbles of thunder can be heard in the west so we decide it might be time to make our way back to home base. As we approach the house we hear the sound of a piano playing. Kate wonders if there's a CD on but I tell her Dad's a whiz on the keyboard. She seems really impressed. She asked if I know the tune he is playing. "That's Desperado by the Eagles," I say.

Dad loves the Eagles. He was given a double CD of the band earlier in the year by the last volunteer teacher I had.

We go into the house and start a good old-fashioned sing-song, not so much with the Eagles music but more so when the Great Australian Songbook is dragged out.

Home Among The Gum Trees, The Road To Gundagai, Click Go The Shears and many more get a real workout. I don't care if I'm was a bit out of tune. It's a lot of fun sharing something with Mum and Dad and Kate. I think we are both a little self-conscious at first but when we get right into it…who cares?

The roar of thunder increases and we catch a glimpse of a few bright flashes through the kitchen window. We go to the front veranda and even though there is a lot of sound and an increasing number of lightning flashes it doesn't have that rainy look about it.

Dad says there is a good chance it will be a dry storm, with lots of noise and the sky being lit up in a spectacular display, but little or no rain.

About a month ago we had a big storm, with the thunder and the light show but also with torrential rain. On that night one of our dogs, a pregnant female called Lady, inherited from our neighbours, took off. She was possibly spooked by the storm, in unfamiliar surroundings and most likely headed for her original home.

We checked with the owners at *Tillenbury*, the property we got the dog from, over the next few days but they hadn't spotted her. We hoped she was safely bailed up somewhere.

Over dinner the noise outside is almost deafening and the lightning so constant there's little need to waste precious electricity on lighting. We all jump up at the same time to the sound of galloping hooves past the house. I see the rear end of Beanie, my horse, heading into the bush. Even though the property has many fenced paddocks and yards, the direction that Beanie's taking is mostly clear of fences. Mum and Dad wanted part of *Kalpago* kept as close as possible to its natural state and that's where my horse is headed. There is no way we are going out to look for Beanie with all that lightning about. Night is closing in so the search will have to wait until tomorrow.

Sleep is hard to come by until sometime after midnight when the thunder fades into the distance and the lightning flashes go with it. I'm not sure about Kate but I must have been well out to it when Mum shakes me in the morning and says it's time for brekky.

I splash water over my face and feel a whole lot better. At the kitchen table Kate looks okay, so maybe she doesn't need as much sleep as me or was able to tune out from the sound and light show last night.

After some cereal, toast and juice we head outside to find out what Dad has planned about finding my horse.

Dad has three horses already saddled up and explains that we have to take things steadily, not only to carefully follow the tracks Beanie may have left but also not to risk spooking her when we find her. There's a chance she may be a bit nervy after her ordeal.

Kate and I hop up onto our horses. Kate is on Matilda, a gentle piebald mare, and I'm on board Rusty, my back-up ten-year old stallion. Rusty is the horse I rode before Mum and Dad got Beanie from my uncle, who runs a cattle property near Hay.

It's not long before we are well and truly into the dense bush. Dad has always been a good tracker, not as expert as many indigenous fellas, but still pretty good. Beanie has left a clear trail for the first two kilometres and then Dad has to use all his skills to pick up the hoof prints in the rockier terrain. I know there's a small clearing a few hundred metres up ahead and I'm hoping this is where we'll find my horse.

So far, we haven't got up to trotting pace, and we now hold back to a really slow walk. The sound of the wind rustling through the trees and the birds singing is louder than our horses. The clearing is just coming into sight and guess what? Beanie is lying down in the middle of the clearing and seems to be preoccupied with something close to her side.

As we get closer Kate says very excitedly, "There's a dog next to the horse".

We quietly approach Beanie and she gets up but still seems to be very protective of the dog.

Dad and I recognised her as Lady, who vanished in the storm last month.

Clever Lady has four pups sucking on her and gives us what seems like a satisfied grin. Maybe that part is just my imagination.

I gave Beanie a scratch on the nose and she appears to be okay after her flight during the storm. Dad suggests he take Lady across his saddle and that Kate and I put a pup in each pocket of our riding coats and set off for home. Dad has planned well by bringing a bridle to put on Beanie to lead her home but I think Beanie would have followed us wherever we were going. Somehow I think she sees herself as some kind of mother to the new arrivals.

9. HOLIDAY ENDS AND THEN WHAT?

Kate's parents arrive late in the morning on the middle Sunday of the holidays. Mum has some salad made up and Dad is busy at the barbeque, cooking up steak, sausages and onions. We eat outside under the giant fig tree on the table and benches that I helped Dad make just last summer.

Kate and I are competing for air space, trying to fill her parents in on our adventures with the poachers and my runaway horse. I leave it to her to tell them about Lady and the pups.

Before she even asks, I can tell she's about to beg them to allow her to take one of the pups home. After all the excitement of our storytelling it seems as if they had a yes ready before she even asks.

Kate is over the moon and gives both her parents a big hug. The only downer is that Kate will have to wait another month to pick up the pup, to allow Lady her full nurturing time with her litter.

They leave mid-afternoon as they have a three-hour drive to their property.

Kate and I are a bit self-conscious when it came to saying goodbye in front of the oldies but somehow at the same time we give each other a big hug. I don't think I have ever felt happier, even if Kate is heading for home. I can't remember a more exciting holiday and I now have a really close friend who likes doing the things I like doing.

There is one week of the holiday left and I'm sure it won't be nearly as exciting as the first. Next term, my last on Distance Ed, I will have a tutor for about six weeks. Mum tells me he is a retired teacher from Victoria, who taught Maths and Science in a Gippsland secondary college. The Maths I'm fairly good at but the Science sounds exciting. We don't get much of a chance to do a lot of Science and maybe he'll bring a few exciting experiments with him. Maybe I'll get to make my own volcano. Maybe term four won't be so bad after all, even considering the great time I've while Kate's been here. Will Kate and I get to spend another exciting time together in one of next year's holidays? I certainly hope so.

JABA'S LAND

"George! George!" Someone is calling. I am often off in my own world and I am not sure for a moment if my name is coming from the fantasy I've been living or maybe from my other life...my real life. It's Mum. I tell her I'm on my way and when I reach the kitchen where the smell of eggs and bacon is coming from, Mum asks me if I've fed the dogs. "About to." I answer, but I know she thinks I've been daydreaming again. I wouldn't say I go off into a fantasy world; it's more like I imagine a "dreamtime" that I've read about in books with stories and pictures of the indigenous Australians and their connection to the land and native animals.

My name is George Clements and the mum who stirred me into action is called Victoria. Dad is John. We live on a cattle property in northern Queensland about 180 kilometres north of Richmond on the Cudgie Creek. That's where the name of our property comes from…it's called Cudgie Springs. Most of the year, from autumn to spring, or from about March to September, Cudgie Creek near our homestead is bone dry. If you can imagine it with water in it, most people would think it is more than a creek, as it is about forty metres across. Right now, it is dry with an expanse of bright white sand with the odd gum tree and evidence of our last flood against the banks and up against some of the trees.

There is no water in the creek near the house, but a couple of kilometres up stream there is flowing water. Does this seem a little weird to you? The first time I saw it I thought something strange was going on. In a way, it is a bit weird. You see, about twenty kilometres upstream the creek is fed by a spring, possibly excess water that doesn't make it into the sub-artesian layer of water, and it flows nearly all the way to our homestead but disappears back into the massive underground water layer. When we get the monsoon rains in summer the small flow of water in the creek is overrun by the fast-flowing torrent that turns Cudgie Creek into the River Cudgie. It hasn't rained heavily for a few years now, but I can remember the time we were cut off for several months. Not only was the creek running from bank to bank but the road into Richmond was cut in quite a few places. Good thing we stocked up just in case and a good thing the cows were still giving us milk and the chooks were still laying eggs.

The September school holidays are starting this weekend and my best friend Sam Davies, from Fog Creek, is coming over for a few days. Fog Creek is another cattle property about a thirty- minute drive further along the road towards Croydon. One of the tutors I had from Victoria thought it was funny that he was coming to a property between Richmond and Croydon. Apparently, there are two suburbs in Melbourne, not all that far apart, called Richmond and Croydon. Maybe you had to come from down south to see the funny side of that. I can't wait for the end of my schoolwork and then a couple of weeks of adventure.

The usual routine on Cudgie Springs is probably nothing like your regular routine, unless of course you live on a large outback property like us with thousands of head of cattle or sheep. As I mentioned earlier, I look after the dogs, both in the mornings before school and in the afternoons just before supper. We have four black and white kelpie/border collie crosses and one pig dog called Buddha. I'm not sure what breed Buddha is, but he is a mean machine when he gets a sniff of wild pig. On the other hand, he is as gentle as a lamb to look after and a real softy when he thinks there is a chance of a scratch on his tummy or behind his ears. The kelpies all have similar markings and visitors often ask us how we tell them apart. Well for starters there are two males and two females, so that narrows it down a bit. The two girls are called Floss and Jess and have slightly different markings around their necks. The boys, Magpie and Tank, have a white patch over opposite eyes. Easy as you like, but still confusing for the governesses, tutors or backpackers until they've been here for a month or two.

Dad milks our two house cows every morning before breakfast. He usually brings in half a bucket which is then filtered through a cloth into glass flagons and put in the fridge. Sometimes we have an oversupply of milk and at other times not so much. Depends a lot on what Mum is rustling up for lunch and supper as well as whether we are in the mood for yummy, cold milkshakes. She also checks on the horses in the late afternoon. Mum likes to keep herself in shape and on Tuesdays and Fridays can be seen pedalling away from the house towards the main road to check the mailbox. That is about four kilometres from the house on loose gravel, so I think that is an excellent way to keep fit. Mustering time is another ballgame altogether as far as work on the property goes. The chores still need be done but it is all bums on horseback for several weeks while the cattle are sorted, tagged and branded. Our current backpacker is a pom called Ben. He is certainly one of the best we have ever had, always willing to do a bit extra and he is really good on a horse too.

Sam arrives tomorrow. Apart from a ride up to the gorge, I haven't put a lot of thought into what we might do. We like doing the same things, exploring and fossicking, so I guess I'll just have to wait and see what we come up with. The last time Sam was here, last year I think, we uncovered an old cow bell beside the airstrip. We couldn't find the strap or chain that should have been with it, but it was still quite a find. Dad polished it up perfectly and it is hanging just outside the back door. During the next few days, we might get lucky again.

Our first adventure, if you can call riding to the gorge and back an adventure, started not long after Sam was dropped off from Fog Creek on the Saturday morning. Even though horses are used on Sam's property, he doesn't ride a whole lot. He prefers to get around on a motorbike. I guess we might be considered a bit old-fashioned at Cudgie Springs but my parents believe working the cattle on horseback is better both for the cattle, and for us in having a good working relationship with anyone who might be helping out with the mustering.

I saddled up Star, my horse since I was about seven, and Dad put all the gear on Domingo for Sam. I once asked Dad why the horse was called Domingo and he said it was because the horse was very "placido". I didn't get his answer then and I don't get it now. Maybe it's some sort of joke. Anyway the horse is very quiet and calm and I'm sure he won't give Sam any trouble.

It's about a two hour ride to the gorge and on the way there are a couple of side creek gullies to negotiate and a few Cudgie Creek crossings to make. From the homestead we followed what might be called a laneway, a three-metre-wide stretch of grey, sandy soil that goes for about a kilometre. Before we reached the creek, there is one shallow gully to get through. I've done this a few times, so Star knows what to expect. Domingo is not so familiar with the gully but he kept Sam on board on the short drop and the half gallop up the other side. Maybe I am being a bit harsh on Sam as he seemed to be handling the riding at this stage very well.

When we reached the running water in the main creek, we followed it for a short distance on the south bank until it was necessary to cross over to a clearer track. In some spots along the creek there are some very, soft spots, what you might call quicksand in the movies. I edged Star into the water to allow him to test his footing and after pounding his hoof into the water a couple of times, he made his way across to the other side. Sam followed on Domingo. The water is only a few metres wide mostly, but in the wet season can be a raging torrent, a couple of cricket pitches across. We are really riding on the river bed for most of our journey to the gorge. There are no regularly running creeks on his property so I got the impression that Sam is really impressed by the crystal clear water in Cudgie Creek. I think the gorge will blow him away.

We let the horses stop a few times to munch on the tuffs of dry grass beside the track. Or should that be; they stopped to munch on the grass while we waited for them to tear off a mouthful.

We made it to the gorge late in the morning and Sam's "Wow! This is fantastic!" meant he was really impressed with the sight of the steep cliffs and their many colours and rock formations. We unsaddled the horses and tethered them with plenty of dry grass to eat.

I love lying back on the sand, looking up towards the top of the cliffs and the bright blue sky. I did just that while Sam took off his boots and socks and went for a paddle upstream. There is one rock shape on the cliff top opposite our usual campsite that looks just like a kneeling man. I imagine him as an aboriginal hunter coming to life and showing me the native ways of catching food and preparing it for eating.

I suddenly realised an aboriginal hunter was now standing over me with spear in hand. He didn't look threatening at all and his eyes seemed to be asking me to come with him.

I heard a "cooee" coming from upstream. Sam was on his way back. I looked around and there was no one within sight. Was I daydreaming again? The man seemed so real. I looked around me for signs of footprints but the sand was so soft it was hard to tell if the dents in the sand were made by us or maybe by someone else.

I answered Sam's call and he appeared around the bend in the creek, beaming from ear to ear.

"This place is more than fantastic," he said. "I even found what looked like cave paintings a little way up on this side of the creek. There were silhouettes of hands and outlines of fish and boomerangs."

I nodded. "Yes, we found them last year. Cool, eh?"

We had cort pots in our saddle bags and a couple of muesli bars each to keep away the hunger pains before we made our way back to home base. Cort pots are double oval shaped metal pots, like little saucepans, a small one that fits inside a slightly larger one. The larger one is used to boil water in the coals of a fire and the small one is for drinking your tea out of. Today we just used the small one for getting a drink from the creek. After munching on our bars and before leaving the gorge we just had to have a dip in the creek. It wasn't summer but it was still close to thirty degrees. The water is only a few centimetres deep for most of its length but there are a couple of spots on bends in the creek where it is waist deep. We found one of these spots and had a great time cooling down and of course splashing each other. I was sure our jocks would dry out, probably even before we got back on the horses.

The horses had had a well-earned rest and chewed up all the dry grass in the area where they were tethered. We saddled up and headed for home. On the way I wondered if I had shown Sam the best Cudgie Creek had to offer on the first day. I kept thinking back to what I had seen while lying on the sand. Was this my wild imagination again? I would have to return soon to find out if I was or wasn't going nuts.

Afternoon smoko was waiting for us when we reached the homestead. Good timing.

That night Sam and I had a bit of trouble getting to sleep. It was mainly Sam's fault because he kept talking about the horse ride and the spectacular scenery at the gorge. I probably wouldn't have nodded off anyway because I was still seeing that towering aboriginal standing over me while I was basking in the sun beside the creek. We must have eventually dozed off as suddenly there was a banging on our door and Mum was yelling "Breakfast is ready".

We quickly dressed and headed to the kitchen. Mum makes great porridge with sultanas and we both put heaps in our bowls. She must have thought we'd need a lot of energy that day as there were scrambled eggs on toast to follow along with some fruit juice.

Mum asked what was planned for the day. We really hadn't thought about it much, but Dad suggested we might try a bit of fossicking for fossils in the old quarry site just off the main road along from our letter box. Even though the quarry has mostly gravel that is used by the council to keep the road up to scratch, Dad said he had spotted a patch of limestone on the northern side which just might be hiding some evidence of the time when this part of Australia was covered by an inland sea. This stretched from the gulf, down through central Queensland, into western New South Wales and then into South Australia to the Great Australian Bight in the Southern Ocean. It retreated millions of years ago and left behind the remains of many animals that either lived in the water or near the shoreline.

The Richmond area is famous for having some great fossil sites. The finds are mainly fossilised marine life such as fish, turtles and squids, but there have been two dinosaur discoveries in the area. They are Minmi, Australia's best-preserved dinosaur skeleton as well as a sauropod, a gigantic plant-eating dinosaur.

We probably wouldn't uncover something as grand as a dinosaur but the suggestion of digging around at the quarry seemed like a good idea to both Sam and me. Dad said he'd drop us off on his way to feeding the cattle in the number one paddock and pick us up mid-afternoon on his way back from helping Johnno at Fog Creek. We packed some sandwiches, fruit and water bottles for lunch and then grabbed a couple of brushes for cleaning off the loose dust and hammers and screwdrivers for levering up the limestone layers. I'd seen Gary and Tim from the museum using those sorts of tools when I went out fossicking with Mum and Dad at the council sites near the town. We added hats and sunscreen to our backpacks and we were on our way.

When we arrived at the quarry Dad pointed out the limestone patch. He headed off in the tilly and we crunched our way over to the digging spot. From what I remembered of fossicking with Mum and Dad, the areas near Richmond are littered with broken rocks and holes where lots of people had tried their luck. Here, the ground was untouched. Sam had been to the council fossicking sites near Richmond like me, so he knew we had to take our time and work as a team if we were to find anything special. We found an area that looked promising and began brushing off the loose pebbles and fine gravel. It seemed that the limestone was in thin layers and they needed to be removed separately. Working side by side, Sam and I had soon cleaned up an area about two metres square. Now came the big test. Could we lever up a layer of limestone without shattering it like a broken mirror? We both got our screwdrivers ready and gently eased them under the edge of the top layer. We tapped the end of the screwdrivers until the limestone started to lift. It was going to be impossible with only the two of us to remove a massive piece of stone, but it seemed like we might be able to get a decent sized bit at least. One final lift and a few reasonable sized pieces came free.

We turned them over and there were a few small reddish-brown patches. From what we remembered these were fish bones or fish spines. There was also a triangular one that may have been a shark's tooth. We would have to check that out later with one of the experts in town. The next layer wasn't quite so intact and was about a metre long and about half that in width. With care, we both thought we had a reasonable chance of removing it in one piece. We started the lifting process again and after about fifteen minutes managed to keep it together. Were we in luck this time? When we turned it over, we both yelled at the same time, "squid!" Yes, on the sheet of rock it was easy to see the outline of a squid with its many tentacles. It was like striking gold. We carefully laid it down, too scared to brush it clean or walk anywhere near it.

We spent another couple of hours fossicking around, away from our "big find" area, and found more small fossils such as bits of turtle shell and fish scales. Dad returned mid-afternoon and couldn't believe we had got so lucky so quickly. Fortunately, he had some hessian bags in the back of the tilly and we carefully placed the prized squid on them. Even though it is not a good idea to ride in the back of utes, I sat guard over the limestone slab, making sure it didn't move around.

After a painfully slow, four-kilometre drive back to the homestead, we placed the squid, affectionately called Simon, on the floor of the work shed. Mum came out and said she guessed we had struck it lucky as the smiles on our faces were wider than the Sydney Harbour Bridge. It seemed that the few days that Sam was with us were turning out to be something special.

Later that afternoon Sam and I had a hit of cricket. Dad had built some cricket nets around a half concrete pitch when he realised I had an interest in playing the game, especially spin bowling. Dad had played a bit when he was younger and provided a good target for my leg breaks and kept most of his bowls on the pitch when I had the pads on. Sam was okay at batting and a fair bowler but had a lot of trouble trying to hit my spinners. After a while I just bowled medium pace to even things up. He was going home the next day and we would have some exciting news to tell whoever picked him up. I also had to try and figure out what I was going to do to clear up the mystery of the Aboriginal hunter I thought I had seen at the gorge.

For a couple of days after Sam left, I helped on the property, going with Dad to check on a pump that was not delivering nearly enough water to one of the tanks. After that there was a bit of fence fixing and we dropped off some lick to a few of the watering spots. Lick is a specially made up mixture that gives the cattle extra nutrients and an extra feed. Suddenly the weekend had arrived and I had been mulling over how to wangle a ride to the gorge to solve my mystery. I decided that making up a reason to go, without telling a porky was the best strategy.

Sometimes honesty is the best policy, at least that is what I had overheard adults saying, and I tried to give it a go, without giving too much away. I asked Mum and Dad if there was any chance I was old enough to ride up the creek all by myself. They answered, after a bit of quiet discussion between themselves that, as long as I took plenty of water and the two-way, it was okay with them. What a relief! I saddled up Star and put a few things in a back-pack; water bottle, two-way radio, snack bars, a knife and a halter to tie up my horse. I started out mid-morning feeling as if I owned the world but at the same time wondering what or who was waiting for me at the gorge.

I followed the same track that Sam and I had used a few days earlier and it seemed like no time at all before I was rounding the last bend in the creek before the steep walls of the gorge and the sandy spot where I had daydreamed and seen my aboriginal hunter.

As I rode up to the same spot a voice came out of nowhere. "Hey Boy! You came back."

I slowly looked behind me, and there he was, my native daydream, but I wasn't dreaming this time. He was as real as the horse under my backside.

"My name's George" I said as an introduction.

"Yes I gathered that from when you were here earlier in the week with your friend." After a few moments silence he added, "My name's Jaba, and this is where my ancestors lived at the time the land started to be worked by the white fellas."

Jaba asked me why I had come back to the gorge so soon after my visit with my friend. I told him about what I thought was one of my daydreams, seeing him standing over me. He said he disappeared when he heard Sam calling out. He he had a feeling I might be looking for something special around the gorge and sharing this with a friend might spoil the moment.

I told him that I had read many stories about the Dreamtime, and for a long time wanted to know more about the life of native Australians living off the land.

Jaba told me a little about why he was at the gorge in the land of his ancestors. He had lived most of his life at Normanton, a community of a little over one thousand people about fifty kilometres from the south-east coast of the Gulf of Carpentaria. It was always in his mind from an early age that he wanted to find out more about the life of the people who he came from. From stories he had been told by the elders at Normanton he had worked out that his people were from the Yanga tribe and lived and hunted around the site of a large gorge with running spring water. Jaba's ancestors had lived on our land many centuries before we tried to make a living from breeding cattle on it.

Jaba had been back in this area for nearly a year and had learnt much about how his people lived off the land and raised their families. He told me he had found several sites which looked like old campsites with evidence of fires and animal bones as well as pieces of rock that were probably parts of hunting weapons or cooking tools. I must have given Jaba the idea that I was entering a special world because he asked me if I wanted to learn some of the things he had been able to teach himself about surviving in the bush.

"Are you kidding? Of course I would!"

He asked if I could make regular visits to the gorge so he could pass on some of the skills he had picked up. How much to tell Mum and Dad? Would they let me repeat my trip to the gorge alone if they knew about Jaba? Would Jaba let me bring them to the gorge to meet him? Jaba said he wanted to pass on the things he had learnt to me and if my parents wanted to be sure I would be safe, then it would be okay to let them meet him. I had the feeling that I was about to start an extremely exciting time in my life.

When I got back to the homestead, I raked up the courage to tell my parents about my trip to the gorge and my new friend. I think maybe they thought this was another example of me being off in my own little world. Daydreaming again. I'm sure they agreed on a ride to the gorge just to satisfy their curiosity about my sanity. Anyway, the next Saturday we rode to the gorge.

I was expecting Jaba to be there but he was nowhere in sight. Mum and Dad were looking at each other and probably thinking, What are we going to do with George? He has to join the real world before it's too late.

I had to do something. I yelled out for Jaba at the top of my voice. I didn't hear or see anything but suddenly a quiet "hello" came from right behind us.

I introduced him to my parents and the questions were flying backwards and forwards at a great rate. Mum and Dad seemed totally taken up by Jaba's reasons for being back home and his plans to teach me some of his skills. It seemed the next part of my life was going to be exciting.

Over the next few months I spent most weekends at and around the gorge with Jaba learning about food gathering, hunting, fire making, cooking and hearing stories he had picked up from the elders at Normanton. I knew this couldn't last forever as next year I would be off to boarding school in Townsville and Jaba had told me that he had set himself two years to learn about the life of his ancestors as part of the Yanga tribe. Living on the property had allowed me to pick up many skills such as mustering, branding, welding and fencing as well as being able to drive most of the vehicles. My time with Jaba had given me something extra, a look into the lives of the people who worked our land before settlement.

I wonder what the future holds for me? Taking over Cudgie Springs when Mum and Dad have had enough or working in some way with indigenous people to try and keep their history alive? Maybe I'll be using some of the skills I picked up from Jaba to give a family of my own a better understanding of what it must have been like a long time ago in this great country.

GEORGE AND THE DYING TREE

Imagine yourself living on a large cattle property in central Queensland. You are twelve years old and doing School of the Air from Charters Towers. My name is George Clement and that is exactly my lot. It's a life that many city boys and girls might dream about… one-on-one school work from a visiting tutor from down south, my own horse and cricket nets next to the house where brother Clancy or dad Bill provide ball after ball to sharpen my skills needed to make the regional under fifteen team.

Apart from all this, I'm faced with a problem. In fact, the whole family is faced with a problem. The on-going drought. The cattle are barely surviving, the nearby Cudgie Creek is down to a trickle and the family members are starting to believe that the good times of recent years are rapidly coming to a dramatic end.

During my early years on School of the Air the Humanities curriculum included some basic lessons about the climate, including the importance of conservation of essential things like water and sound use of the land. One of my assignments in Year Three was to plant a gum tree that was sent out from the school as a seedling and to nurture and monitor its growth. This sparked a keen interest in me to not only think about my special tree but also to think about the importance of doing things on the property to get the best out of the land.

Now four years later, even though my tree is still alive, it is showing signs, like much of the property, of dying. Thoughts start rolling around in my head and I can't help connecting the survival of this tree with the survival of the farm and Mum and Dad's future.

Earlier in the year, when my closest friend Sam came over from Fog Creek for part of the school holidays, we went on horseback up the creek about nine kilometres to the gorge and as you already know, that is when I met my friend Jaba.

That was many months ago, and I wondered if Jaba might still be at or around the gorge or if he had gone back to his regular life in Normanton.

I wondered about that a lot, so, after a few weeks I talked Mum and Dad into letting me do another ride up to the gorge on my own. After the ride up the creek, I lay on the sand at the gorge, just as I did on the trip with Sam.

A voice boomed from behind me. "Hey boy! You came back again!"

I slowly looked behind, and there he was, my native friend from earlier in the year.

Jaba had showed me many of the ways of his ancestors in looking after the land, making sure that plants and animals were treated respectfully, even though they were used for food and shelter.

I told Jaba about my gum tree back home that was struggling to survive in the harsh drought. Jaba said that the climate worked in cycles and similar conditions had happened many times before. The elders of his clan had told him that. The secret to reviving my tree was to have a strong connection to the land and to make the tree believe that I have a strong love of it and the environment generally.

So simple? Well, I hoped so! Over the next few months I made several trips to the gorge, meeting up with Jaba and learning more about the importance of connection to the land and the power it possessed.

I spent many hours trying to think of ways to help my tree recover its old self. I tidied up the area at the base of the tree and set some small plants at its base, like those that would have been its companions if it was out in the bush and not a few metres away from the cricket nets.

Jaba said that talking to the tree might be good in helping it to recover. I had heard Mum say something about gardeners talking to plants like flowers, fruit and vegetables and believing that this was a way to help get more out of the crop. I tried this, even if a bit self-consciously at first over several weeks and the tree seemed to be gradually getting better. It had shinier leaves and even grew a little taller.

One night, I had just put down the book I was reading and switched off the bedside lamp, when I heard a distant rumble. It had been a long time since I'd heard a sound like that and I hoped that soon I would hear noises on the roof signalling that the drought may be finally over.

It started with a few heavy plops and then turned into something much heavier. It was pouring! I liked to think that my positive thoughts about looking after my tree and having an improved connection to the land had something to do with the change of fortune for my tree, the property and the surrounding countryside.

Deep down I knew there was only a touch of truth in all this but still I believed that what I had learned from my friend at the gorge would be valuable for me and also to those who make decisions about the land in their comfortable offices. There had to be better ways to look after our special country and not do things when thinking only of money. I wanted them to shift their thinking towards the future that I hoped to have when I was a parent and beyond.

THE ADVENTURES OF ELL AND CEE

Ell and Cee live on a big, in fact massive, sheep property in western New South Wales. Just to make sure you are clearly in the picture, New South Wales is a state in Australia, squashed between Queensland to the north, Victoria to the south, South Australia to the west and the Pacific Ocean to the east.

Anyway, back to our two heroines. If you manage to make it to the end of this story you will find that they are two very brave girls. By the way Ell is ten years old and Cee has her thirteenth birthday coming up in a couple of months.

If you live in a city or a large country town it may be hard to imagine just how big their property is. *Kalyanka* covers about five hundred square kilometres and is home to over six thousand sheep.

As you might expect on an outback property the girls have many animals to look after and enjoy playing with. They have their own horses and are surrounded by dogs, chooks and pet lambs.

Even though every day has the feel of an adventure about it, Ell and Cee do manage to fit a few hours of home schooling into their busy routine.

Kalyanka stretches to the distant low range but near the homestead the property lies on the banks of the mighty Darling River. The river at this point has steep banks and is home to a large variety of wildlife, namely fish, birds, emus and kangaroos.

The girls have chores to do each afternoon after school, including feeding the animals and collecting firewood. At the time of this story, the river had been in flood after many years of drought. Before that, the river had been little more than a series of puddles and struggling to maintain its reputation as one of Australia's mighty rivers.

On this sunny, spring afternoon the girls are on the riverbank collecting wood washed down by the floodwaters when Ell notices what looks like a large log floating downstream. As it gets closer Cee realises it isn't a log but an upturned canoe. The girls decide, almost at the same time, that maybe they can get it to shore and see what sort of condition it's in.

Cee races up to the work shed and grabs a long rope. Back at the river the canoe is nearing their spot on the outside of a bend and just might get close enough to snare. Ell suggests tying a piece of wood to the rope. This is quickly done and Cee tries to lob the weighted rope over the canoe.

As the missile hits the water, missing by the narrowest amount, Ell thinks she hears a noise coming from the canoe. Cee's second attempt goes right across the upturned boat and together they manage to carefully inch the canoe to the shore.

What a surprise when the canoe is turned over. Wrapped up in rope from the canoe is a life-jacketed man mumbling something that sounds like "thanks".

The girls manage to get him to the bank and, even though he's shaking, he manages to tell them he got caught under the canoe when it flipped after hitting a river snag.

The man tells them his name is Kenny Grant and he is one of four canoeists in training for the World Championships later in the year. The girls help the man up the bank and across to the homestead where their mum gets the surprise of her life seeing her daughters with a bedraggled and wet stranger.

The rescue story is quickly related to Mum with the girls competing for air space, followed by a phone call to let Kenny's friends know he is okay, although a little sore and embarrassed about capsizing the canoe.

The next day the girls become heroines as their names are splashed across the front pages of most major newspapers telling of their rescue of Australia's champion Iron-Man Kenny Grant.

In the minds of many Australians the girls are certainly brave and quick thinking, but they have more important things to think about. The Wentworth Show is coming up in two weeks and getting Silky and Elphaba preened and ready for the chook competition and practising on Nimbus and Della for the equestrian events are their top priorities. Rescuing a careless canoeist was just another everyday *Kalyanka* adventure.

JOHNNY MAKES GOOD

J ohnny knew he had a problem. In fact he had one problem which led to another problem. Johnny loved to have a beer. Most of the time this didn't cause any hassles for him or those around him. For many years, he had worked on a number of outback cattle and sheep stations doing whatever jobs were needed, whether it was fencing, mustering, branding or helping out in the maintenance shed.

Riverside, on the banks of the mighty Darling River in western New South Wales, was his favourite place to bed down and enjoy the wonders of the Australian outback and the hospitality of the owners Mick and Billie. Bedding down was probably overstating Johnny's accommodation. After the evening meal was over and everyone had enjoyed a quiet ale around the massive log fire and the outside telly, Johnny slept rough. Well rough for anyone who was used to a nice warm bed in the homestead or central heating in the town or city. Johnny slept in his swag a few hundred metres away from the main house. There were shearers' quarters available but he loved the wide open spaces and the freedom to spend time staring in amazement at the brilliant canopy of stars overhead before he drifted off for a well-earned six or seven hours of shut-eye, ready for another tough work day.

Now having a quiet beer or two around the fire of an evening is one thing, where there was always pleasant company and stories to tell about the day's work or more likely exaggerated yarns about exploits from the many yesterdays. Most weekends Johnny wangled a lift into town, about fifteen kilometres from the *Riverside* homestead, and this is where his problems arose on a regular basis. In town at the local pub, Johnny didn't just have a few quiet beers. He had his weekly pay packet and drank way beyond his limit and this inevitably led to an argument and ultimately a fight with someone who was usually a bit stronger and hadn't had as much to drink as he had. The publican made every effort to nip these blow-ups in the bud, but Johnny always seemed to get under his guard, and this usually led to Johnny being escorted to the door and told to make his way home. Sometimes he was lucky enough to have someone drop him off at the *Riverside* gate but usually footing it back was the only option.

Mick and Billie knew the value of Johnny for the efficient running of the property but were concerned for his welfare, both in the town and when he got back to doss down out on the flats. A couple of times Mick found him of a Sunday morning, not even in his swag, but sound asleep on the open ground. There was lots of scrap material in and around the property and Mick came up with the idea of building Johnny a shack with a few luxuries like a bed but more importantly, a roof over his head.

So began the project of building Johnny's shack. Timber was gathered, along with corrugated iron and a few items scrounged from the tip, such as a bed and mattress and a discarded cupboard. Mick, being very handy with most tools, had no trouble constructing the outer walls and roof of the shack. The need to make sure this small room would stay standing in the strong winds that sometimes sweep across the treeless flat plains got Mick thinking about something substantial for a front door. He remembered a dead river gum about a kilometre along the river that had an unusual gap at its base. That could be made into a unique entry and provide the rest of the building with something solid to keep it upright. The tree came down and provided many great logs for the evening fire. It also, with a little artistic magic from Mick and his trusty Stihl chainsaw, gave the shack one of the best entries to a building you are ever likely to see. I guess you might say it was the outback equivalent of those concrete portals at the front of the McMansions in the big cities. It was literally amazing. You stepped through the tree opening to the door just beyond and into a small bedroom on a dirt floor.

Johnny now had a roof over his head and even though he still slept out under the stars on very hot nights, he did appreciate the gift of a roof over his head on those chilly outback nights and on the rare occasion of a much-needed downpour.

Mick and Billie had two children, Toni and Michael Junior. Both these youngsters were very resourceful for their ages, Toni was fourteen and Michael was five. Young Mick was in his first year of distance education through the Broken Hill School of the Air and Toni was about to head off to high school after completing year eight. Whereas Toni was good at her schoolwork, producing some amazing projects, and very capable on the piano, young Michael was full of adventure. He loved nothing better than to be sitting on the fence when the mustering was being wound up in the yards or on the back of the four-wheeler when his mum had to go out and check on the sheep in the far paddocks. He had to be kept under close watch in case he got into a dicey situation.

One lazy Sunday afternoon when Johnny was soaking up the sun outside his shack, he noticed a big, red kangaroo about a hundred metres across the flats munching on a tuft of grass. Johnny was marvelling at the sight of this magnificent animal when he caught movement of something out of the corner of his eye. It was young Michael heading straight for the kangaroo, seemingly unaware of the danger. Johnny rushed after Michael and managed to grab him just as the big red was shaping up to lash out. The kangaroo didn't seem to see Johnny coming or hear his yells but appeared to be fixated on the young boy.

When Johnny grabbed Michael, the kangaroo bounded off towards the scrub on the riverbank.

Billie saw the tail end of this drama and rushed over to thank Johnny and give Michael a big hug. In the days that followed Johnny thought long and hard about the importance of life and how lucky he was to be looked after by such a loving and caring family. Following the rescue and his days of deep thought, Johnny rarely went into town, unless it was with Mick and Billie to the golf club for a meal and a night of bingo or trivia. He made the most of the quiet times; having a family meal, drink and a yarn around the nightly log fire.

DARLING DONE OVER

Arrived at Riverside to find the river bone dry,

Even a visitor had a good reason to cry.

Walked along the riverbed of grass and sand,

From somewhere on high, it needs a big helping hand.

Now and again there are environmental flows,

A bit of water passes and then it goes.

Water leaves Queensland through Bourke and Louth,

But not much at all makes its way down south.

Big cotton growers are bleeding it dry,

One needs to ask the big question…why?

Illegally taking much more than allowed to,

Not taken to court by the powers that knew.

This once mighty river can thrive once again,

With a sound plan and some good soaking rain.

ABOUT THE AUTHOR

 Greg Jessep is a retired secondary teacher of Mathematics and Science and lives in the Latrobe Valley in Victoria, east of Melbourne. Since 2010 he has ventured into the remote outback areas of Queensland and western New South Wales to tutor upper primary and lower secondary students doing their schooling via Schools of the Air. The stories in this book have been inspired from his time on these outback properties working with amazing young people and their supportive and resourceful parents.

ABOUT THE ILLUSTRATOR

Ester de Boer is an artist, author, and children's book illustrator based in Gippsland, Victoria. She loves creating illustrations with imagination, humour and unexpected detail that keep the reader looking back. You can view more of her work at www.esterdeboerillustration.com